Bye Bye Baby

by

Allan Guthrie

First published in 2011 in Great Britain by
Barrington Stoke Ltd
18 Walker Street, Edinburgh, EH3 7LP

www.barringtonstoke.co.uk

ISBN: 978-1-84299-873-1

Printed in Great Britain by Bell & Bain Ltd

Part One
Frank

Tuesday
Mayfield Square Police Station, Edinburgh

1.

I was on my way downstairs to grab a can of something fizzy from the drinks machine when I passed Detective Sergeant Dutton's office. I made the mistake of looking up. He saw me and waved me over.

His room was tiny. The desk took up most of the space and it wasn't a big desk. I wondered how DS Dutton managed to pull the chair out far enough to squeeze himself in. He was a beefy guy with a porn-star moustache, which he stroked as he listened to the caller on the other end of the phone.

I stood in the door catching the faint smell of fag smoke from Dutton's clothes.

He scribbled a few notes, grunted something, then said goodbye and hung up.

"You can have this case, Collins," he said to me. "Missing kid."

"You serious?" I said. "I can have it?"

Dutton didn't like me.

Last time I saw his wife, I told her she should leave him. She told him what I'd said.

Yeah, I know, I should mind my own business. But I'd heard the way he spoke to her and it was ugly. I'd happily do the same again.

"Why wouldn't I be serious?" he said. He pulled a face in an attempt to look hurt. "Well, if you don't think you can handle it ..."

I clenched my teeth. "How old's the kid?"

"Seven."

"Where's the mother right now?" I asked.

"At home."

I nodded. "You got the address?"

"Right here." He tapped a scrap of paper on his desk with his pen. "You sure about this now?"

"You think I'm not up to the job?" I held out my hand for the paper.

Issu

Branch:Ware Library
Date: 24/02/2021   Time:
Name: Baldock, Charlotte
ID: ...0605

ITEM(S)	DUE DATE
Summoning the dead 52504432 Item Value: £7.99	03 Apr 2021
Bye bye baby 463080596 Item Value: £5.99	03 Apr 2021

Total value of item(s): £13.98
Your current loan(s): 3
Your current reservation(s): 1
Your current active request(s): 0

To renew your items please log
onto My Account on the OPAC at
https://herts.sp,dus.co.uk

Thank you for using your local
library.

But he just chewed the inside of cheek and peered at me. "Maybe it ne someone more senior to run it," he said. think I should take it."

He knew I'd been after a big case for ages. I'd decided a couple of months back that if I didn't get promoted in the next year, I was going to get out of the police force. No way I was going to stay a DC forever. Too much paperwork and overtime and too many arseholes like Dutton. I had bills to pay, or I'd have left already.

I said, "You decided yet?" If Dutton wanted me to beg, he'd have a long wait.

We stared at each other for a while. Then he said, "Don't make me regret this, Collins," and handed over the address. "The mother's spoken to Uniform," he said. "I'll get her statement. Fill you in over the radio."

"I can speak to Uniform when I get there," I said.

"I've already sent them door to door," he told me. "Need all the bodies we can get out there looking for the kid." He pointed his

...e. "One other thing. There won't
...tim Support Officer free for about an
...You better take a female passenger
.. you."

"You left the mother on her own?" I said,
...nocked.

The Scottish police do almost everything
in pairs. You'd think we'd have partners like
on TV cop shows, but no. You just find
whoever's available and take them along. In
our office, we called them 'passengers'.

"She picked a bad day to lose her son,"
Dutton said. "We're busy. But she knows
we're on the way. She'll be fine." He pushed
his chair back, gave himself just enough leg-
room to get to his feet. "Now bugger off and
show me what you can do."

2.

The office where us lowly DCs worked
was open plan, with pale wood desks
separated by 30-cm-high partitions on legs.
We all kept moving them when nobody was
looking. Everybody wanted that extra inch

4

or two of desk space.

I glanced around, hoping to spot one of the female officers but there were none to be seen. Hell, I didn't need to drag a woman along anyway. I'd be fine with a bloke. We could deal with a mother who had lost her kid. She would be upset, of course, and it'd be hard to begin with, but we'd cope.

Two male officers, Moore and Temple, were in the kitchen area in the corner, making coffee.

I caught Moore's gaze and nodded towards him. He ignored me and turned to Temple.

I wasn't surprised.

God knows what I was thinking when I joined up. When Holly and I first got married, I was a bus driver. Enjoyed that more than any other job I'd done. Then she got pregnant and we got by for a few years. Then she got pregnant again and we knew we were going to struggle so I applied for the police. No big deal.

After I'd been in uniform for seven years, I put in for CID. They turned me down. The next time they turned me down too. Third time, they took me. Thanks to my uncle, so I heard. I don't deny that he was a big help.

Becoming Detective Frank Collins was a major step up in my career. But it didn't take long to see that I wasn't going to get any further.

My uncle told me I had to keep my mouth shut and learn to kiss some arse. Two skills I didn't have.

I scanned the office again, still looking for a passenger to take with me. One guy I hardly knew was sitting at his desk, making a call. The only other officer around was DC Erica Mason.

I hadn't worked on a case with Erica in a while. I'd been trying to avoid her. Or she'd been trying to avoid me. Maybe a bit of both.

I walked over to her desk and cleared my throat.

She looked up from her computer screen, her olive-green eyes wide. She reached behind her head and smoothed her ponytail. Her hair was dyed, dark red. Her nail polish matched her hair.

"Why do I feel as if I'm not going to want to hear this, Collins?" she asked.

"We might have a missing kid," I told her.

She nodded. "And you want me as a passenger?"

"For the mother's sake," I said. "It'll be easier for her to talk to a female officer."

"That's a load of shite," she said.

"Just grab your jacket," I told her.

She glared at me. "I didn't say I was coming."

"Erica, the boy's only seven," I said.

She took a deep breath. "What's his name?"

3.

The boy was called Bruce Wilson. He lived in a three-bedroom detached house on a quiet street in the Blackhall area of Edinburgh. As we pulled up I took note of the well-kept garden. The burglar alarm.

The shiny red Range Rover parked in the drive.

There was no sign of the uniformed officers Dutton had sent to speak to the neighbours. I wondered where they'd parked. At least one patrol car should be out in the area too, using a megaphone to ask if anybody had seen the boy. We hadn't passed it on the way but it would be out there somewhere, driving around. Those were the steps we followed. Dutton would have seen to it. No matter how much I hated him, I couldn't deny that he knew his job.

The boy's mother, Mrs Wilson, opened the door before we reached the end of the path.

"Are you the police?" she asked. She was 31 years old, according to the file Dutton had passed me. But you'd have guessed at 40. She wore a light jumper, jeans, sandals. Her face looked as if the skin was being stretched tight over the bones. Her eyes were wet and red. She winked at me, which was odd. I wasn't sure whether to wink back or ignore it. Then she winked again and I realised it was a twitch.

I told her who I was. Erica did the same.

Mrs Wilson looked into Erica's eyes and said, "I'm so glad to see you."

She led us inside.

The sitting room had red walls. And a red ceiling. It should have been too much but it was a big room and the colours worked. There was a lot of light, too, from the bay windows. Picked up the shine from the floor. Bare wooden boards. A big rug that looked like it cost a fortune lay in front of a green and silver marble fireplace. The sofa and chairs were white. And spotless. I was impressed she could keep them so clean with a kid around. Bet she had a cleaner in a couple of times a week to give her a hand. No question she could afford it.

Mrs Wilson invited us to sit down on the sofa. We did, to put her at ease. She sat down too, crossed her ankles and uncrossed them again.

Erica perched on the edge of the sofa, opened her notebook and said, "In your own time, Mrs Wilson. Would you mind running through what happened one more time?"

Mrs Wilson looked at her feet. "I went to pick up Bruce from school." She lifted her head. Her gaze moved from Erica to me, then back to Erica. Then back to the floor. "He wasn't there."

"Where do you usually pick him up?" I asked.

"No," Mrs Wilson said, with a shake of her head.

"No?" I repeated.

She shook her head again. "Not usually," she said, her voice louder. "Always. I always pick him up outside the school gates. I'm always there when the bell rings."

"And he wasn't there today?" Erica asked.

"That's right."

"He wasn't in his classroom?" Erica said.

Mrs Wilson breathed in slowly. Didn't answer the question.

"Maybe one of the other parents could have ...?" Erica didn't finish the question.

Mrs Wilson was shaking her head wildly

again. Erica bent over and scribbled in her notebook.

I wondered if I should say something. After all, it was my case. I was about to speak when Erica asked Mrs Wilson, "How can you be so sure? About the other parents?"

"I stay out of their business," said Mrs Wilson. "They stay out of mine."

"What do you mean by that?" I asked.

Erica pursed her lips like she was annoyed with me for cutting her off.

"Nobody wants to hear about grief," Mrs Wilson said. "People want to get on with their lives and that kind of stuff holds you up. Even if it's someone else's grief. It can infect you like some kind of disease." She laughed but her eyes were dead. "Surprised no one's asked me to wear a bell round my neck so they hear me coming and they don't have to deal with me."

I gave Erica a look.

"What grief do you mean," she asked Mrs Wilson. "What happened?"

Mrs Wilson gave a deep sigh.

"If you don't mind telling us," I said.

"Talking about it doesn't hurt quite so much now," she said. She looked up from her hands. "John died," she said. "Bruce's dad. He died."

The officers who spoke to her first must have told Dutton about this and he should have let us know. I wouldn't be surprised if he had kept it back on purpose.

Mrs Wilson was talking again. "It was a car crash." She put her hands over her eyes. "Head-on." She lowered her hands, gripped her legs. "The other driver was drunk. He took a corner on the wrong side of the road. Killed John."

"I'm very sorry to hear that," I said. "How old was Bruce at the time?"

"It happened seven years ago in March," she said. "Bruce was just a baby. Eight months old."

I looked at Erica again but she was no help. I asked, "Do you have a photo of Bruce, Mrs Wilson?"

"He doesn't like cameras."

"It doesn't have to be a good photo," I said. "Anything will do. Just so we know what he looks like."

She said it again, slower this time. "Bruce doesn't like cameras."

"You don't have any photos?" I asked again. She must have given one to the Uniforms. "Just one – "

"He doesn't like having his photo taken," she said. Then maybe she thought she'd been a little loud so she looked at her feet and said it again, softly.

"What about a school photo?"

"What is it you don't get?" As she stood up, Mrs Wilson banged her shins against the coffee table. But she didn't seem to notice. "I won't put Bruce through anything that upsets him. I won't do that. He's suffered enough, losing his father. Can you imagine what that's like? I know he's too young to understand, but the older he gets, the more it shows and he acts up and ... and I let him, I suppose. Maybe I spoil him a bit. But he hurts. I know. I feel it." She started to cry. Big messy tears, runny nose. She wiped her

13

face with her hand.

Erica pulled a tissue from a box on the coffee table and handed it to her.

Mrs Wilson blew her nose. "My boyfriend says Bruce comes between us. Can you believe that? Blaming my baby?"

"What's your boyfriend's name?" Erica asked.

"Les. And he's my ex-boyfriend." Mrs Wilson dabbed at her nose. "I got fed up with him being so jealous. I finished with him last week. Told him to leave us alone. And that's what he's done."

"Les who?" Erica asked.

"Green. Les Green."

"Do you have his address?" I asked. She told us it and Erica wrote it down.

"I'm sorry to have to ask this," I said. "But did your relationship with Mr Green end on good terms?"

She shook her head. "He called me a 'mad bitch'. But he didn't raise his hand to me. If that's what you mean."

"Could Mr Green have picked up Bruce

from school?" I asked.

"He wouldn't dream of it."

"I think we should talk to him anyway," I said.

"Whatever you think."

We sat and stared at each other for a bit. Then Erica said, "Could we see Bruce's room?"

"Why not." Mrs Wilson got to her feet, led us down the hall and up the stairs. She swung a bedroom door open and stepped inside.

We followed her in. It was a little boy's room. Piles of books in the bookcase, games stacked in the corner, toys in their boxes. But there were things I would have expected to see that weren't here.

"No TV?" I asked.

"I don't like him watching too much of it."

"Computer?"

"He's not old enough to be interested."

"Really?" I said. "My two were into computers from before they could speak."

"You've got two boys?" Mrs Wilson looked me in the eye and there was no sign of the twitch.

"Yeah," I said. "Older one just had his thirteenth birthday. His brother's ten."

She looked as if she was about to ask something else, but Erica broke in. "Have you tidied up in here?"

"No need. Bruce is a neat little boy."

"Very," Erica said. "Is anything missing? Clothes, maybe? Money?"

"Money?" Mrs Wilson leaned back an inch or two, her head to one side.

"I just wondered," Erica said. "Kids sometimes have a bit of cash stashed away."

"Not Bruce," Mrs Wilson said. "He doesn't need money. What would he need money for? I have money."

"Clothes?" Erica's voice was calm but firm. "Any clothes missing?"

Mrs Wilson shook her head.

"Can you take a look, please," I said. "Just to make sure?"

"For God's sake." Mrs Wilson pulled out

the drawers, scanned through the wardrobe. A couple of minutes later, she crossed her arms and said, "Everything's here. Apart from what he's wearing."

"And what was that?" Erica asked.

Mrs Wilson told us he was wearing his school uniform, which she described, and then told us about the Hearts scarf he liked, but wasn't allowed to wear in class. It matched the info we'd got from Dutton. At least he'd got something right.

I asked Mrs Wilson, "There's not one single photo of him?" I wondered what Uniform were working with. Just a description of the boy?

She looked as if she was going to leap across the room and choke me. But instead she said, "John was the upbeat one."

I had no idea what she was talking about. She must have seen how confused I was.

"Bruce's dad," she told me. "My husband. Remember?"

I nodded. "Yes, yes, John, of course," and I'm sure I sounded like a total idiot. I hadn't forgotten her husband's name. I just didn't see how her reply had anything to do with my question about Bruce's photo.

But who knew how her mind was working right now?

"You know what it's like not being able to say sorry?" Mrs Wilson asked, her fists balled up tight. "We'd argued, me and John. Just before … It was a silly thing, didn't know it would become important. He hadn't shaved for a couple of days."

I ran my thumb over my chin.

"I asked him if he was growing a beard." She started pacing around the bedroom. "He was already stressed out. Hard day at work with a major client. I didn't realise how stressed he was until he told me to shut up. Told me to stop nagging him." She was walking up and down, pumping her fists. "That was the day before the crash. And I never apologised to him, and now I can't tell him I'm sorry. Can't tell him that he looked just fine." She smacked her fists against her legs. "I don't give a crap about him not shaving. I was a total fool! I've lost John. I can't lose Bruce too."

"I think you should go back downstairs," Erica said. "Sit down. Relax. And please don't jump to conclusions about Bruce."

"Yes." Mrs Wilson cupped her hands over her nose. "OK. I think I need a drink."

4.

Outside, I called Dutton on my Airwave handset. I hated those stupid big things and would have much rather used a mobile phone.

"There's no sign of any activity round here," I said. It was true – there was still no patrol car, no Uniforms talking to neighbours at their doors. "What's going on?"

"They're spreading out," Dutton said. "Kid's still missing."

"What do you want us to do?" I asked.

"School's closed and everybody's gone home for the day," he said. "Bruce's teacher, name of ..." there was a pause "... Mrs Grace Lennox, lives about five minutes away. No one's spoken to her yet. Pay her a visit."

He gave me the address. I told him about the boyfriend and Dutton said he'd get Uniform to go round to check out Mr Les Green and make sure Bruce wasn't there.

"By the way," I said, "did anybody get a photo of the kid?"

"Why wouldn't they?" he asked.

I told him what Mrs Wilson had said.

"She must be upset," he said. "Uniform got a photo no problem. I'll see if I can get you a copy."

"And what about the car crash?" I asked. "Her husband's death?"

"What about it?"

"You didn't tell me," I said.

"I didn't? Must have slipped my mind."

And before I could reply he was gone.

5.

In a couple of minutes, we were outside Bruce's teacher's flat. She lived in the last stair of a tenement block with the date it was built carved into the stone above the door. 1881. It was a nice enough area but not as leafy as the one we'd just left.

"There's a kiddie fiddler a couple of doors down," Erica said. "Real sicko."

"Once they're out, they have to live somewhere," I said.

"He was never locked up. The dirty sod got off with it."

"Lack of evidence?" I asked.

"Yeah, and he was smart. Wouldn't talk. Right from the off, all he ever said was, 'No comment'."

"You think there's a chance he might have followed Bruce's teacher to school?" I asked.

"Now that you mention it." Erica nodded slowly. "Maybe we should pay him a visit."

"Right after we've spoken to Mrs Lennox." I pressed the buzzer and a man's voice answered. "Police," I said. I'd always enjoyed saying that.

6.

Upstairs, Mr Lennox was waiting for us at his door. "How can I help?" he asked. He wore heavy-looking black-framed glasses and he couldn't stop smiling.

He didn't seem nervous, though. More likely he was just eager to please. That happened more often than you'd think. Sometimes people made up all sorts of stuff just to try to help us out. One time this old dear described a burglar to me in great detail, all the way down to his ginger beard and nose ring and Hibs top. Turned out she never saw the guy. She just wanted to help and she reckoned that's what a burglar would look like.

"Could we speak to your wife, sir?" Erica said to Mr Lennox.

"She just popped out for some milk," he said. "But she has her phone with her. I can give her a call." He raised his eyebrows to ask Erica if he should.

"Please do," Erica said. "Tell her we'll meet her outside."

We trotted down the stairs and back out into the street. The late afternoon sun still had some fight left in it. Shadows dappled the roof of the pool car.

We waited by the side of the road.

A couple of minutes later, a heavy woman came jogging up the road. She wasn't dressed for running. And she was carrying a carton of milk.

"I think this is our girl," I said.

We walked towards her.

"Mrs Lennox?" I said.

"Officers." She put her hand on her ample chest and breathed hard through her open mouth. Her eyebrows were plucked too thin and made her look a bit startled. "How can I help?"

"It's one of your pupils," Erica said.

"Oh. Who's been up to what?"

"It's about Bruce Wilson. He's missing."

Mrs Lennox laughed. She sounded like a smoker.

"Why is that funny?" I asked her.

"You're having me on."

"I can assure you, Mrs Lennox, that this is extremely serious."

She coughed twice and stared at us. "Call me Grace, please," she said. "'Mrs Lennox' makes me feel like I'm at school and we don't want that. I'd have to ask you both to put your hands up before you ask a question."

"Grace," I said. "We've just spoken to Bruce's mother. Is there anything you can tell us?"

"I didn't need to run after all."

"What you mean by that?" Erica asked.

Mrs Lennox nodded. "You'd better come on up."

7.

The sitting room was full of family photos. On the walls, above the fire, on the furniture.

I sat down and Erica sat beside me.

"OK." Mrs Lennox took a rattly breath

and wiped her hair out of her face. "It's like this."

And she told us about Bruce Wilson.

8.

"Were you in on this too?" I asked Erica once we were outside.

"In on what?"

"Dutton knows," I said. "He set me up."

"If that's true, then that shithead set me up too." She ground her teeth. "Maybe the teacher's lying," she said.

But we both knew that wasn't the case.

I punched Dutton's number into my Airwave handset.

"The hell are you playing at?" I asked when he picked up.

"Found wee Bruce yet?" He chuckled. "Sorry. I couldn't find that photo after all."

"Dutton," I said. "You're a total disgrace."

"Any decent detective would have found

out about the kid long before now."

I hung up. "I'm going to kick his head in," I said to Erica.

"Not if I get to him first," she said.

9.

"Where are we going?" Erica asked me a couple of minutes later. We were in the car.

"To talk to Mrs Wilson," I said.

"What about Dutton?"

"I need to calm down before I see him." I gripped the steering wheel. "He can wait."

10.

"Don't go stomping all over this," Erica said as we stood at Mrs Wilson's front door.

"What do you mean?" I asked.

"Go easy on her."

I banged my fist on the door. Again and again. There was a bell, but screw that. I liked the pounding noise. "Mrs Wilson?" I shouted. "Mrs Wilson!"

"Collins!" Erica grabbed my arm.

I clamped my jaw shut, pulled my wrist away and pounded on the door some more. Finally Mrs Wilson opened it.

I stared at her, wondering what the hell went on inside her head. "Can we come in?" I said. I could smell the drink off her.

She walked ahead of us. Slowly. As if she was afraid she might fall over. In the sitting room, she asked if we'd like a cup of tea.

Erica said no.

"Coffee?"

"Nothing to drink, Mrs Wilson," I said.

"We're fine," Erica told her. "Thanks."

Mrs Wilson picked up some bottles off the table. Whisky, vodka, something else. They all looked empty. She held them there for a moment and then put them back down again in the very same spot.

I glanced at Erica, hoping she'd say something. I didn't know where to start. But Erica just raised her eyebrows at me.

Mrs Wilson crossed her arms over her chest in the shape of an X. Her voice was steady, no trace of slurring. "Is it bad news?" she asked.

"To tell the truth," I said, "it was a bit of an eye-opener." I couldn't tell what she was thinking. "We spoke to Mrs Lennox," I said.

No reaction.

Erica said, "She told us about the accident, Clare."

Clare. Not Mrs Wilson. For crying out loud, Erica.

"An accident?" Mrs Wilson whispered. "Bruce has been in an accident?"

Erica shook her head. "Mrs Lennox told us how you and John and Bruce were all in the car that night. Seven years ago."

"Yes," Mrs Wilson nodded. Kept nodding. "What does that have to do with Bruce being missing?"

"Mrs Lennox told us how ... John ... how John died on impact," Erica said.

Mrs Wilson put her hand to her mouth. Held it there.

"She told us how you suffered terrible injuries and almost died."

"But here I am." Mrs Wilson took her hand away from her mouth and smiled, although her lips trembled. That twitch in her left eye was back too. "My skull was shattered," she said, as if that was something that happened every day. "They said it was a fine old mess in there. But I'm as good as new now, see?"

"Mrs Lennox also told us about Bruce," Erica said.

"She told you what? She knows where he is?"

Erica looked away.

"If they know where he is, you have to tell me." Mrs Wilson stepped forward. "Take me to him. Please."

I'd found it hard to believe what Mrs Lennox had told us and what Dutton knew before he sent us out, but now Mrs Wilson's face made it all very clear. If you were looking for batshit crazy, Mrs Wilson was a bat with more shit than most. I wasn't angry with her any more. I couldn't be. But I couldn't let her keep this up either.

I said, "We did consider charging you with wasting police time."

"Wasting your time?" she said. "My son's gone missing! You're supposed to help me find him. Isn't that what you do?"

Damn it, maybe it was none of my business, but it had to be done. Somebody had to spell it out. "Mrs Wilson," I said, "your son was in the car the night you were hit by the drunk driver."

For a moment she looked confused. Then she said, "I know. I know. Me and John and Bruce. We were all in the car."

God help us. I took a deep breath. "Your son died that night."

"Sweet Jesus," she said. "Sweet Baby Jesus. Ask for help and this is what I get?"

Erica moved towards her. "Bruce died that night," she said. "It's true."

It was. We even knew where the boy's grave was.

"What is this?" Mrs Wilson asked. "You think saying it enough times will make it real?" She wiped her eyes. "I think you should go."

"Is there anybody we can call for you?" Erica asked.

"I really think you should go. Now."

"Mrs Lennox said you were seeing someone," Erica said. "A psychiatrist. Would you like to speak to – ?"

"Get out. Get the hell out."

"We're just trying to help." Erica stretched out a hand, but Mrs Wilson batted it away.

"You pair aren't the first," Mrs Wilson said. "And you won't be the last. But you're wrong. My baby's alive and well. I make him a packed lunch every day. I take him to school. I pick him up from school. I take him to the park. I play with him. I have dinner with him. We talk about his daddy. I bath him. I put him to bed. I read him stories." Her shoulders were shaking. "The bond we have," she said. "It's special. And nobody's going to break it."

Erica and I looked at one another and turned to go. There was nothing more we could do here. I was so depressed my knees hurt.

"Clare," Erica said. "You need help."

I grabbed Erica's arm, tugged her towards the door.

"I'll find Bruce on my own," Mrs Wilson said. "I'll find him. I will."

I had no doubt she would.

11.

I entered the code to the security door that led to the CID office and stepped inside. Erica was right behind me.

Cheers and claps and wolf whistles greeted us from the bunch of detectives who'd gathered to welcome us back.

So word had got out that we'd been played. I'd reckoned that Dutton would have kept it to himself. I was wrong, of course. The whole point of a joke was to share it.

And there he was, leading from the front, big grin under that stupid moustache.

I stepped towards him but Erica got there first.

I wondered what she was going to say.

"Want to see something really funny?" she asked. She made a fist and punched him.

He went down, and stayed there. After a moment's silence, the cheers and claps grew louder.

12.

My uncle, DI James Fleck, was crouched in the corner of his office like a large duck. His hair was straight and as white as his shirt and a bit too long at the front.

"Come on in and shut the door," he said.

I was expecting a bollocking since I didn't stop Erica belting Dutton. She'd been sent home. It was hard to find a good way to look at striking a superior officer. No matter how much the superior officer was asking for it.

"Your back still no better?" I asked my uncle.

"Come over here," he said. His teeth were bared against the pain.

I walked past his desk in too much of a hurry, bumped it, made a photo of my Aunt Sarah wobble.

"Whoops." I caught the photo before it fell and put it back beside a photo of my uncle's boat. Lucky I hadn't knocked that one off or there would have been big trouble. He'd had to sell the boat a few years back and my Aunt Sarah had said you'd think he'd been forced to sell one of his children, the fuss he made about it.

"Never mind that," he said. "Take one of your shoes off."

My uncle had strange ideas sometimes. Although he hid it well. Still, almost everybody was scared of him. Even his superiors. And they thought I would be too. Which is why they moved me here.

"Come on, sunshine," he said. "I'm not asking you to flap your cock in my face. Just take a fucking shoe off."

I bent down, unlaced my shoe. Slipped it off. I stood there, feeling unbalanced.

"Good." My uncle waddled in a tight circle so he was facing the other way. "Now put the sole of your foot in the small of my back."

I raised a bent leg and let my foot rest on his shirt. "There?"

"Just a bit higher."

I moved my foot up a bit. Slipped for a moment. Then steadied myself.

"Super." My uncle stretched his arms out behind him. "Now grab my arms."

I took hold of his arms.

"Lean back and pull," he said.

I said, "I don't know about that."

"Shitebags. Just do it."

"OK." I puffed my cheeks out. Then leaned back and tugged.

He yelled. He kept yelling.

I kept pulling as I leaned back. "Want me to stop?" I shouted over the noise he was making.

"No, keep doing it."

"You sure?"

"You fucking deaf?"

I had a good mind to let go. Let him spring forward and headbutt the wall. But I didn't.

"That's better," he said after a while.

I relaxed my grip a bit.

"No, no, no," he said. "Keep the pressure on."

I dug my heel into his back.

"Ah," he said. "That's good. Yes. Keep it there. Fuck, yeah."

I said, "This is becoming a little too sexual for my liking."

"Very funny," he said.

"You getting any proper treatment for this?" I asked. He'd had a bad back for as long as I could remember. It sort of came and went.

"I'm seeing a specialist tomorrow," he said. "Another one. Costs me a fucking fortune."

"Any closer to knowing what's wrong?"

"They won't tell me," he said. "That's the way they like it, of course. More cash for

them while they 'find out'. Let's try this.
Oh, it's not that. Then let's try this instead.
Oh, dear. Not that either. Well, let's see ...
Meanwhile, I'm so skint I can't
afford to put a few quid on the horses any
more."

"You'll find a way."

"You sound like your aunt," he said.

"Just stating a fact," I said. "You won't
let it stop you. Am I right?"

"The more that bag gets on at me, the
more I'll bloody do it," he said. "She tells me
to stop gambling. Gambling. I don't fucking
gamble."

"You don't?" I asked.

"Course I don't," he said. "I'm a betting
man. Gambling's a lottery. Odds are against
you. But a betting man looks for value.
Only plays when the odds are good. Your
aunt should know that. Old bag's been
married to me for God knows how long. She
doesn't listen." He leaned forwards. "No
bugger does, mind you. Keep the pressure
on, eh?"

I got a better grip on his arms.

"Ah, yes," he said. "Oh, that's nice. See, a gambler will take any odds. If you're a gambler, gambling's the thing. Fucking profound, I know. Now a betting man, he's cleverer than that. A while back there was a football match on. European game. And I got a tip that one of the bookies had screwed up. There was a defender and striker in the same team who have similar names. And the bookies had listed them the wrong way round. Both Bulgarians, you see. Funny names. So, anyway, the striker's odds of scoring the first goal were 20/1. And the defender, he was listed as 2/1. There's your fucking clever bet. I stuck a shitpile of money on the striker. 20 to fucking 1 when the real odds are nearer 2/1? You hardly ever get value like that, sunshine."

"How much did you win?" I asked.

"Not a penny. Some other fucker scored first. But the rule still holds good. It was still a value bet. You get enough of them, and over time you'll come out on top. But you have to take some hits along the way. That's what your aunt doesn't understand. You get it?"

"Totally," I said. "Makes perfect sense." And in a way, it did. Can't say I fancied trying it, though. I'd rather keep my money.

"Good," he said. "You can let go and put your shoe back on now."

My leg felt stiff. I gave it a shake.

He turned, still in a crouch.

I slipped my shoe back on. "You need a hand?"

"I'm more than capable of standing up," he said. I watched as he eased himself to his feet. Looked painful.

"Is that all?" I asked him.

"No," he said. "The Wilson case. Sergeant Dutton claims there was a mix-up and the right information didn't get through to you. That so?"

"No," I said. "It very much isn't."

"He was fucking with you, I know that," my uncle said. "And while you may be a fanny now and then, it doesn't mean Dutton should get to slip you a length."

He had a way with words, my uncle.

"Thanks," I said. It wasn't normal for

him to support me. He was mostly harder on me than anybody else. Just in case anybody started shouting about favourites.

"I've sent DS Dutton home as well," he said. He cleared his throat. "But I don't want to lose him. I promised I wouldn't say anything, but there's something you should know."

"Tell me," I said.

"His wife left him."

I felt myself smile. I said, "I'm sorry to hear that," but I knew I didn't sound like I meant it.

"Don't be a shite, sunshine," my uncle said. "Look, I don't want to lose Dutton. Any more than I want to lose Erica. They're good cops."

"One of them is," I said.

"I'll be the judge of that. My job, not yours."

I nodded. "What's Erica saying?"

"She says Dutton could be right," he said. "There was a bit of a mix-up."

I was surprised to hear that.

40

"She wasn't so sure at first but I convinced her after a while," my uncle said. He stretched, pulled a face. "Do you think I can convince you?"

"I doubt it."

"Bad reception, maybe?" he suggested. "And you missed hearing about the kid having died seven years ago?"

"I don't think so."

"It's a possibility, though?"

"No."

"Pity," he said. "Cause if that were the case, then we could get this mess sorted out no worries. You don't want Erica to lose her job, do you?"

"She punched a superior officer. Not much I can do about that."

"She's apologised," he said. "Dutton's accepted. We'll find a way back for her."

"And Dutton gets off the hook for wasting police time?"

"With a warning," my uncle said. "He'll be demoted next time. And if he fucks with you again, I'll punch him myself."

"OK." I nodded. "That seems fair."

"Super."

"Is that it?" I asked.

"Just one more thing. It's your Aunt Sarah's birthday next week. Any idea what I could get the old bag?" He stretched, winced. "Nothing too dear."

13.

That night, I was at the kitchen table with Holly, topping up her glass of nice French white. We were having a late dinner, which I'd cooked. When I say 'cooked', I mean I'd stuck two packets of pre-prepared chicken tikka in the oven and boiled some extra rice. Tasted pretty good, anyway. The boys had eaten earlier with their friends and were out playing football.

Holly and I had the house to ourselves for a while.

I'd just finished telling her about Bruce Wilson and his crazy mum. About Dutton. About how he'd made me feel. I'd hoped

Holly might comfort me a bit.

But she just gave me a blank stare. Hazel eyes, caramel skin, which the boys had inherited from her. They all tanned. I burned.

She took a sip of her wine, licked her lips.

I had stuck with beer. Wine and curry didn't work for me.

Holly said, "Will Erica lose her job?"

The reason I hadn't worked a case with Erica for a while was because we had some history between us. Me, Erica and Holly, that is. The three of us had slept together. First time was when Holly suggested a threesome one drunken night, and Erica said OK, it'd be a giggle. No need to ask what I said. But I can't say I'd enjoyed it much. It wasn't much fun being ignored.

Holly and Erica were right into it, though.

Second time, they slept together without me. Didn't ask or let me know.

I don't think Holly would have ever said

anything about it if she hadn't got drunk and angry one night. She gave me more details than I needed. I'd never said anything to Erica but I could tell that she knew I knew. Holly must have told her.

Sex had never been the same between me and Holly since. In fact, these days we hardly slept together. And when we did, half the time she fell asleep before we were finished. The other half of the time, I did.

"You like to go to bed with her again?" I said.

"Oh, for crying out loud." She leaned her head back, her eyes shut tight.

"I'm only asking," I said.

Her head snapped forward, eyes open, shining. "Why won't you shut up about it?"

"I don't know," I said. I didn't.

"Just let it rest," Holly said. "I've said sorry till I'm hoarse. What more do you want from me?"

I reached across the table and took hold of her hand.

"Would you like to sleep with her

again?" I asked. "Answer me."

"Would you?" She pulled her hand away.

Thursday

14.

Mrs Wilson's shrink was called Dr Snow. She greeted me at the door to her office with a walking stick and a cute smile. If she'd been twenty years younger I'd have said she was flirting with me. Maybe she was.

She limped over to one of the two chairs in front of her desk. "Please," she said, and pointed with her stick.

I took the free seat.

"Thanks for coming." She moved her stringy grey hair out of her eyes. "It's kind of you." She smoothed her skirt.

"My boss sent me," I said. "But I admit I'd like to hear what you've got to say."

"Indeed, Mrs Wilson's case is... curious." She smiled again, so the skin around her eyes creased. "She called me this morning in a terrible state."

"Bruce hasn't come back?" I grinned but Dr Snow didn't grin back.

"You know, officer, that Bruce has gone missing before?"

"Twice," I said. Oh, yeah. I'd been told all about it.

"And you know he turned up after a couple of days?"

I nodded. Dutton had known Mrs Wilson was a nutjob all along. All he'd done was send around a couple of Uniforms to calm her down and then I'd walked past his desk, so he'd decided to have some fun at my expense.

I doubt he thought it would get as far as it did, though. Never expected he'd get to make such a monumental fool out of me.

"This time it's different," Dr Snow said. "There's been a development."

I waited, no idea what was coming. My uncle had just told me to get over here pronto, that the shrink would provide the details. And that I was to report to him after.

"Mrs Wilson has received a demand for money," Dr Snow said. She paused. "Two hundred and fifty thousand pounds, to be precise."

"Oh, that's beautiful," I said. The crazy woman had written herself a ransom note. "She's totally lost it."

"Well, I think it's a natural progression," said Dr Snow. "And if you think about it, it's not a bad thing."

"How can that be?" I asked. "It means she's getting worse, no?"

"On the surface, that's how it might look," Dr Snow said. "But I think it might be her way of letting go at last." She leaned towards me as if she was going to tell me a secret. She even lowered her voice. "I believe she's tried before." Her breath smelled of strawberries.

"The previous disappearances of her son were an attempt to let go of the belief that he was still alive," she went on. "But it was too easy for him to come back. Maybe she needs to add a kidnapping and ransom demand.

47

Maybe if she doesn't pay it, something will happen to Bruce and ..." She spread her fingers.

"And this time he doesn't come back?" I asked.

She nodded, sat upright.

"OK, I get all this," I said. "But why did you want to speak to me?"

"It's important that Mrs Wilson follows this through. She told me about your partner, DC Mason."

"Erica, yes."

"DC Mason kindly gave me the name of DI Fleck. Said I should talk to him."

"And you did and he sent me along," I said. "I'm second best, then."

"We have to use what we're given." She smiled again. "He spoke very highly of you."

"That's because he's my uncle."

She started to laugh.

"It's true," I said. "He is. And he has to say nice things about me or my mum gets angry."

"I see," she said. "But joking aside, none

of us want Mrs Wilson to pay the ransom."

"Can she afford to?" I asked.

"She's a wealthy woman," Dr Snow said. "Her husband was a partner in a major law firm. And he had invested his money well. When he died, he left her quite a bit. The house was paid off. And there was insurance money too. I've no doubt Mrs Wilson could pay the ransom several times over."

"I'm a cop, Dr Snow," I said. "And I'm not sure this is police work."

"Despite what your uncle says?"

I nodded. "I solve crimes. That's my job."

"Then at least check it out," Dr Snow said.

"But there's no crime here."

"Mrs Wilson says she has a ransom note," Dr Snow said. "Is it not a crime to demand money from someone?"

"We know she wrote it herself."

"Do we?" Dr Snow asked.

"If she didn't, then who did?"

Dr Snow smiled. "Like I said, you should at least check it out."

15.

Fifteen minutes later I was in Mrs Wilson's sitting room.

"Can I see the ransom note?" I asked her.

"No."

Her response surprised me. She'd seemed pleased to see me when she opened the door. She looked older today, the stress in her face clearer. The twitch in her eye was regular now, every few seconds.

"It's evidence, Mrs Wilson." I dug in my pocket, took out my notebook. "I need to see it."

"You can't." She looked through the bay windows at the empty street outside. "I tore it up."

I couldn't control myself. I said, "For God's sake."

She turned her face away from the

peaceful scene outside. Placed her right hand on her left shoulder and rubbed as if the muscle was sore.

"I'm sorry," I said.

"He told me to."

"Who did?" I asked.

"The man who took Bruce."

"Mrs Wilson, are you sure there was a note?"

She put her hands on her head and pressed down. She rocked backwards and forwards a few times. "It was on a sheet of A4," she said. "Folded in three. The words were made out of letters cut out of magazines. Or newspapers."

Just like the movies. These days, most ransom notes were typed up and printed. But Mrs Wilson wasn't to know that.

"What did you do with the pieces?" I asked. "When you tore it up?"

She lowered her hands. Crossed her arms. "Set fire to them."

"Where?"

"In the sink," she said. "Then I washed

the ash away."

"So there's no trace of it?"

"None."

I said, "Do you mind if I sit down?"

She shook her head, sat down in the armchair and crossed her legs. I sat across from her. She uncrossed her legs and leaned forward.

I didn't know what to say to her. "Can you tell me anything about the ransom note?" I asked, in the end.

"The envelope was white," she said. "There was no name, no address, no stamp. He must have put it through the letterbox."

"This morning?" I asked.

"Maybe last night. I don't know."

"What time did you go to bed?" I asked.

"I don't know," she said again. "I was out late, looking for Bruce. It wasn't here then. I had a couple of drinks after that. Only way I can get to sleep."

"Do you still have the envelope?"

She shook her head. "I thought I should burn it too."

"Pity," I said. "What did the note say? Do you remember?"

"Every word."

"Tell me," I said. "Slowly, if you don't mind."

I noted down the words as she spoke them:

Mrs Wilson,

Sorry about this but I need the money.

250 grand in cash by Friday night.

Deliver the money and I will deliver your son.

I'll tell you where.

Burn this letter after you've read it.

"That's it?" I asked.

"Yes."

"Word for word?"

"Yes. I knew I was going to have to get rid of it so I memorised it."

"He didn't use Bruce's name?"

She shook her head.

That was interesting. And what I'd expect from a real kidnapper. Most of them didn't refer to the victim by name.

"And it didn't tell you not to contact the police?" I asked.

"No," she said. "If it had I wouldn't have let Dr Snow call you."

That was odd. Most ransom notes said to tell no one. I would have thought Mrs Wilson would have known that, but maybe she had left it out on purpose. Maybe she wanted Dr Snow to get in touch with us. Could be the shrink was right and Mrs Wilson was looking for help to come to terms with her son's death.

"When I spoke to Dr Snow," I said, "she had the feeling you were going to pay up."

"Of course I am," she said. "I've spoken to the bank. I pick up the money tomorrow."

"They were OK with that?" I asked.

"I spoke to the manager," she said. "Told him it was a family emergency."

"Still, I'm surprised."

"He wasn't keen," she said. "Told me it

couldn't be done. But I'm a good customer. I let him know that he didn't want to upset me or I'd take my money and find another bank. He changed his mind then. Suddenly he couldn't be more helpful."

Yeah, I was sure that it would be more than his job was worth to lose an account like Mrs Wilson's in the current financial climate. "I'd advise you not to pay," I said.

"You can't stop me."

"That's right," I said. "If you want to give your money away, that's up to you."

"It doesn't matter to me," she said. She got to her feet. "I want my son back, whatever the cost."

"OK," I said. "I know you do."

I could have used Erica's help right now. It was unfair of my uncle to send me here on my own. What made him think I could deal with crazy people? I found sane people hard enough.

"I know what you're thinking," Mrs Wilson said.

I didn't think so. "What's that?" I asked.

"What if I pay the ransom and Bruce still doesn't come back?"

"That is very likely," I said. It really did sound as if she was trying to find a way to kill him off at last.

"It's a chance I have to take."

What annoyed me was that she'd probably go and leave the money in a random spot in the middle of nowhere and some passing tramp would pick it up. Screw that. If she was determined to give her money away, there were other people who could use it. Me, for instance.

OK, it crossed my mind, I admit it. But only for a second or two.

But then it crossed my mind that it might have crossed someone else's mind too.

Dr Snow had said it. If a ransom note existed, we didn't know that Mrs Wilson had written it herself. Why go to the bother of writing a note and then burning it?

God, this was a mess.

If Mrs Wilson was determined to hand over her cash, there was only one way I could think of to stop her losing it for good.

"Mrs Wilson," I said. "When you hear where to deliver the money, let me know. Could be dangerous. I'll deliver it for you."

"That's very kind," she said. "But I've already had an offer."

16.

"What can I do for you, officer?" Les Green asked.

I liked to think I could keep an open mind, but I'd already decided Mrs Wilson's boyfriend was an utter scumbag before I even met him.

He looked harmless enough. An inch or two over six feet, friendly smile, relaxed. He had strange hands, though. I noticed when he held one out for me to shake. His fingers were bent, as if they'd been broken and not re-set. Or as if someone had given his hands a few hard smacks with a hammer.

Not the sort of hands you'd think a photographer would have.

Mrs Wilson had given me his address, an artist's studio in Stockbridge.

They'd made up last night, she'd said. It was all back on.

Les Green's studio was the end one of five. It was a small space, and it looked even smaller with all the clutter. The walls were covered in framed photographs. Most were portraits. There was one of Mrs Wilson, looking lost.

The grey carpet on the floor was like something you'd get in a prison. There were a couple of big lights on tripods, a black umbrella thing and a white disc to reflect light. A wide strip of white cloth ran down from a ten-foot-high board and ran across the floor for another ten feet or so. Different cameras and lenses lay about the place. A dozen empty frames leaned against the wall and magazines littered the floor.

I gripped Les's hand. "What do you call that big white sheet?" I asked.

"An infinity backdrop." He tried to pull his hand away. "It makes it seem as if the person in the photo is standing in space."

"Interesting. And is this your job or your hobby?" I already knew which it was. Mrs Wilson had told me. But Les didn't know that.

I squeezed his fingers.

His face didn't change. "I worked for the local rag for a few years," he said. "Got laid off a couple of months back. Decided to take some time out. Work on my own projects. Wanted to see what I could do if I had a bit of time."

I let go of his hand.

He held his hands out, spread his fingers. Each one was twisted to the side, or back the way, at the tip or middle joint. Freaky as hell.

"You'd need to squeeze a lot harder," he said, "if you wanted to hurt me."

"Why would I want to hurt you?" I asked.

"I was wondering the same thing."

I stared at him for a bit, then said "Listen, I don't mean to be rude. But, your fingers. Is that some kind of bone thing that

59

makes them bent like that?"

He laughed. "No, cricket. I used to be a wicket keeper."

"You must have been pretty bad."

He clenched his fists. His right index finger stayed out over his thumb. He spoke, his voice soft: "No, I almost made the national team."

"Not a lot of competition, I suppose," I said. "Cricket's not the most common sport in Scotland. Surprised you even managed to get a team together."

He took a step back, put his hands by his sides. "Clare said you were coming." The softness had gone from his voice. "She didn't say you were a prick."

"Nice." I gave him a couple of slow nods. "Ballsy."

He looked at me.

"And stupid, of course," I said. "Sums you up, don't you think?"

He took a long breath through his nose. "What do you want?"

"So you're unemployed?" I asked.

"Self-employed," he said.

"Making any money?"

"Not yet."

"You rent this place?" I asked.

"Yes."

"Make the rent OK?"

He gave me a look. "What did Clare tell you?"

"Mrs Wilson told me she pays the rent for you."

"It was her idea," he said. "She insisted on it."

"And you just can't bring yourself to say no," I said. "Probably upset her too much and you wouldn't want to do that. Am I right?"

"She wants to help me out. I'm not too proud to let her."

"Right," I said. "Funny thing, you know. I got the feeling she didn't like photos."

"Because of Bruce?" he asked. He shook his head. "It's odd, but the more you get to know her, the more you realise how real Bruce is to her. It's Bruce who doesn't like having his photo taken. She doesn't mind."

"All a bit confusing, isn't it?" I said. "Why didn't you get your fingers fixed, by the way?"

"Thought I'd lose my place in the team. Wanted to keep on playing."

"You played with broken fingers?"

"Only one at a time."

"Not just ballsy and stupid," I said. "But hard as well. My mistake."

"We all make mistakes," he said. "Don't be too tough on yourself."

"And you think you're witty, too," I said. "A fine list of personality flaws."

"Can we get back to the subject?" he asked.

"And impatient," I said. I moved forward a little. "Can I speak frankly?"

"Like I could stop you."

I put my hand on his arm. "Your personality stinks, Les. Makes me think the worst of you."

He shook my hand off.

"OK, you're right, "I said. "We should

talk about Bruce. Good idea. My understanding is that you claimed he was spoiling your relationship with Mrs Wilson. I can understand that. Nothing like a dead child to mess things up. Never mind a dead child who's come back to life."

He said nothing.

"And so you and Mrs Wilson broke up," I said. "But now you're back together?"

"We patched things up," he said. "I said I was sorry."

"Once you heard about the kidnapping."

"I love her." His voice went soft again. "You've met her. It's impossible to be with her. But I do love her."

I didn't believe him. Not for a second.

"And because you love her," I said, "you offered to take 250 grand in cash from her?"

"She's going to throw it away."

"And you want it for yourself."

"No," he said. "I want to make sure she gets it back. The only way I can do that is if I'm the one who delivers it."

"Ah." I couldn't fault his logic. It was

the same as mine. "So you're thoughtful as well. I like a man who's thoughtful, Les. In fact, I like it so much I'm going to help you. How about I give you a hand to deliver the money, eh?"

"What do you mean?"

"I'll come with you," I said. "Tag along behind in my car. Make sure everything goes OK."

He looked at his hands, stretched those bent fingers. "And then what?" he asked.

"You'll go away and tell Mrs Wilson it's done."

"And leave you with the money?"

"You don't trust me, Les? I'm offended."

"What's to stop you keeping it?"

That was a very good question.

17.

I'd hardly set foot back in the station when my uncle called for me.

I walked passed Dutton's office. The door was open but it was empty. At the end of the corridor, I stopped and knocked on the door marked 'Detective Inspector James Fleck'.

He shouted for me to come in.

I wondered if I'd find him on the floor and we'd have to go through that foot-in-the-back stuff again. I really wasn't in the mood.

But he was sitting at his desk, looking comfortable enough.

On the other side of the desk was DS Dutton, stroking his moustache. I caught the familiar whiff of stale smoke.

"What the hell's he doing here?" I asked my uncle.

"Shut up and pay attention," my uncle said. "I want you to behave. I want both of you fuckwits to behave. Any more crap and I'll come down on the pair of you so hard, you'll be shitting out your own fucking heads."

His outburst caught Dutton by surprise. The poor dolt's mouth fell open and the hand that had been playing with his moustache hovered in the air like it didn't know what to do with itself.

"I didn't do anything," he said, and his hand fell.

"And I can knit cardigans with my cock." My uncle rubbed his chin. "Look, you don't like each other, that's fine. Just shake hands and get the fuck along. I don't have the time or the energy to dick about any more. OK?"

Dutton looked at me and held out his hand.

I took it. His palm was sweaty and cold. We shook.

"Super." My uncle clapped his hands. "Now get out."

I turned to go.

"Hang on, sunshine," he said. "You stay. I want an update on the loony mother."

Once Dutton had gone, I said, "What about Erica? Is she coming back soon?"

"I invited her to come back," he said. "But she said no. She's decided to leave."

18.

I was at home when the call came in. I'd been thinking about heading to bed, where Holly had gone a couple of hours earlier. The boys had fled to their rooms to play video games after dinner and left me alone.

I hadn't been able to sit around doing nothing, so I'd gone out for a drive. It helped me think. By the time I got back home, though, I wasn't sure what I'd been thinking about.

Right now it was just me and late-night TV and that ringing phone.

I didn't recognise the caller's number, so I let it ring out.

A minute later it started again.

This time I checked to see if there was a message.

"Detective Collins." It was Les Green's voice – the last person I expected to hear from. "Something's happened," his voice said. "Can you call me back?"

I called him back. "What is it?"

"Well," he said. "Well, it's a finger."

19.

"I don't get it," Les said.

We were in Mrs Wilson's kitchen. Me and Les were standing by the worktops. Mrs Wilson was sitting at an enormous dinner table, downing a bottle of single malt.

"Why would someone send a finger?" Les asked. "Is it some kind of warning?"

"That's possible," I said. "It's standard in kidnappings."

"Only if the family doesn't pay up, though," Les said. "Clare was going to pay up."

Which was true. And there was no note to explain. No demands for money, nothing. Just a finger in a clear plastic bag. It had been dropped through the letter box within the last couple of hours.

I'd spoken to the neighbours who still had their lights on. Nobody had seen or heard anything.

"It's a sick joke," I said. "This whole thing is."

The finger was fake, of course. It looked

real at first. Your eyes went to the blood right away, and only then did you notice the colour and feel of the finger was wrong.

It was something you could pick up in a joke shop. Something Mrs Wilson could have picked up in a joke shop. Also something Les could have got hold of. But what I didn't get was why either of them would do such a thing. There was nothing to gain. And Les really did look baffled. I had to admit that.

"This finger," I said to Mrs Wilson.

She wiped her eyes. Took a sip of whisky. Nodded.

"You know it's not Bruce's," I said.

"Course I do" she said. "I'm not stupid. It's made of rubber and it's far too big."

"Yeah," I said, my voice sarky. "That's why it's not Bruce's."

"Don't," Les said.

I looked at him.

"Just don't, please," he said, and I saw that his eyes were full of tears. He walked round the table and sat next to Mrs Wilson.

He put his arm around her.

I wanted to think it was for show, but I was beginning to think Les Green wasn't such a scumbag after all.

20.

I called Erica on the way home.

"You woke me up," she said.

"Yeah, but listen – "

"You sodding well woke me up."

"You should come back to work," I said.

"What's it to you?"

"You can't let Dutton win."

"That's not why you rang," she said. "What do you want?"

"I need your advice," I said. "I've got nobody else to talk to."

"Jesus, Collins, I'm not a cop any more."

"Of course you are. You can't just walk away."

"Watch me."

"But you know the score," I said. "You know the case. You've met Mrs Wilson. I just want to talk it over. It's not making any sense."

"Talk it over with your uncle."

"Come on," I said. "I can't wake him up at two in the morning."

She yelled down the phone and hung up.

I gave it five minutes and called again. But the phone rang out. I got the answer machine. "Hey," I said. "I miss you. Come back."

She didn't call back.

I drove home with the fake finger inside a plastic evidence bag on the passenger seat.

Friday

21.

It was about 9.30 when I drove to Mrs Wilson's. The sun was out and it felt like the wrong kind of weather.

I'd swung by the station at seven.

Dropped off the fake finger, wrote a short report.

I hadn't slept much. I reckoned Mrs Wilson wouldn't have slept much either. I was right. She came to the door in the same clothes she'd had on last night. Looked like she hadn't even gone to bed.

She looked rough, but then I'd never seen her look anything but.

"I have a few things to check out," I said. "Can't stay."

"Who is it?" Les's voice in the house behind her.

"Have you heard anything from the kidnapper?" I asked Mrs Wilson.

She winked at me, then shook her head.

"When you do, call me," I said. "Right away."

"OK."

"It's important. That business with the finger," I said. "We can't be too careful."

Les came and stood behind her. He was dressed too, with his keys hanging on the end of his index finger. He gave me a look and said, "Still don't trust me?"

I wasn't sure what he meant.

"Then tag along," he said.

22.

I followed them to the bank. It was one of those private banks in the West End. I went inside with them and had a seat in a posh waiting room. Then we got taken to a private room the size of our CID office where we were offered tea and coffee.

We all refused.

The manager arrived and shook hands with us all. His face was scrubbed clean and he stank of aftershave. Reminded me of a pimp I'd once arrested.

"Is my money ready?" Mrs Wilson asked.

"On its way." The manager rubbed his hands together. "Now," he said, "are you sure I can't get you to take a cheque instead?"

"No," I said, and showed him my ID card.

"Ah, OK." He took an envelope out of the pocket inside his jacket, opened it, and gave Mrs Wilson a form to fill in.

We tried to make small talk while we waited for the cash. But nobody felt like saying much and after a bit the chat stopped and we sat in silence.

The money came in a charcoal-grey briefcase with the bank's logo stamped in gold on the front. There were couple of security guards on each side of the clerk who brought the money.

"Thanks." Mrs Wilson got to her feet. "Can we leave now?"

"Goodness, no," the manager said. "We have to count it to show you it's all there."

"No need." Mrs Wilson turned to the clerk and held out her hand.

"I'm afraid it is," the manager said. He took the briefcase from the clerk. "With a sum this large, we have to insist on it. Mistakes can easily be made."

"I suppose that's going to take a little while," Les said.

"I'll get some help." The manager opened the case and started taking out packs of £50 notes. "But, yes, we're probably talking thirty minutes or so."

"See that coffee you offered us?" Les said, steering Mrs Wilson back to her seat. "We'll maybe have some after all."

23.

As it happened, the coffee had just arrived when I had my uncle on the radio.

"Sounds like you had a wild night," he said.

I gave him a run-down of what had happened.

"You on top of it, sunshine?" he wanted to know. "Need any help?"

"Don't suppose Erica's changed her mind and come back?" I asked.

"She's gone," he told me. "Forget about her."

"Then I'm fine," I said.

"Super. That's what I like to hear."

I was flattered he trusted me to run this on my own. "I'd planned on checking a few things out," I said. "But I don't want to leave the boyfriend alone with Mrs Wilson. Not when he could just walk off with the money."

"Think he will?"

"No," I said. "I don't think so."

"Then go check out the things you wanted to check out," my uncle said. "If he fucks off with the money, we've got our man. I kind of hope he does. See how far he gets before we nail his hairy hole."

"But ... " I started.

But my uncle was right. I could leave them for a few hours. The drop wasn't taking place till this evening. And if Les was behind all this, then I couldn't read people at all.

"Any chance you could get some Uniforms to ask around, see if any of the neighbours saw someone hanging about Mrs Wilson's last night?" I asked.

"Who would be hanging about?"

"The guy who put the finger through the letterbox."

"Surely he'd have dumped it and buggered off."

"Maybe, but it's worth checking, don't you think?" I said.

"Thought you did check, sunshine? Last night?"

"Nah," I said. "I just dropped by a couple of houses where the lights were still on."

"So you're sure someone stuck this finger in Mrs Wilson's letterbox?" he asked. "You don't think she bought the finger herself and made all this shit up?"

"It's possible," I said. "We won't know that till we find out who picks up the money. If anybody does."

"Tonight's going to be fun," my uncle said. "Want some company?"

24.

I spent the morning checking out the local joke shops to see if any of them sold the kind of fake finger Mrs Wilson had been sent. Turned out they all did. But none of them had sold any in the last few days. I'd need to do a bigger search.

I was on my way to grab a sandwich when my mobile rang. It was Les.

"Clare's gone," he said.

"What the hell do you mean?"

"She told me she was hungry," he said. "She said she wanted some beans on toast and cheese. That's about all I can cook. So I went to make it. When I came back, she wasn't here."

I waited a second. "And the money?"

"Gone too. She's taken it with her."

25.

I was staring at the plate of toasted cheese and beans on the table in Mrs Wilson's house, wondering if it was too cold to eat, when Control called to tell me Mrs Wilson's Range Rover had been found. Dumped, less than five minutes' drive away. No sign of Mrs Wilson yet but Uniform was checking door-to-door.

I gave Les the news.

He stared at his hands. "What do you think that means?"

"The kidnapper probably told her to leave the car," I said. "Get on a bus. Grab a taxi, who knows? He must have known we'd try to find the car and follow her."

"I never expected this," Les said. He walked over to the window. "When she said she was hungry, I believed her. She hadn't eaten a proper meal since ... I don't know when."

"Don't blame yourself," I said. "This guy's smart."

"Maybe we're just stupid."

"That's always possible."

"What can we do?"

It was a good question, but one I didn't have an answer for. "I'm going to get out there and help look for her."

He stared out of the window. "She could be anywhere by now."

"We have officers all over the place," I said. "Someone will find her."

He turned. "I'll grab my coat."

"No," I said. "You stay here."

"I want this guy." His eyes shone. "I want to see what kind of person would do this to Clare. I want to break my fingers on his chin."

"And I need you to wait here," I said. "In case she comes back."

26.

I hadn't meant to fall asleep, but my eyes were too heavy to keep open so I'd pulled into the side of the road just in case.

The news on the radio must have woken me. Control repeated it and what I heard was like a pint of iced water down the back of my neck.

They'd found her.

27.

Mrs Wilson was standing in front of the school gates. Bruce's teacher, Mrs Lennox, was with her. And so was someone I didn't think I'd see again. Not at work, anyway.

I parked and got out of the car.

"I don't want to talk to anybody," Mrs Wilson was saying. "Leave me alone."

Erica looked at me and raised her eyebrows.

"Miss me?" I asked her.

"No," she said, "I just decided you were right. I couldn't let Dutton win."

"Good to have you with us again."

I said hello to Bruce's teacher, then turned to Mrs Wilson. "Where's the money, Clare?"

"Leave me alone," she said.

"Please," I said. "Tell me where the money is." It was almost certainly too late. Wherever it was, the kidnapper would have picked it up by now.

"Not till Bruce is safe. I've already told her." Mrs Wilson nodded at Erica. "I'm not

81

saying anything till my baby's back." She looked at her watch. "Five minutes. Wait five minutes. He'll be here then."

"That's great," I said. "Maybe while we wait, you could tell me what happened. Les was worried."

"Les doesn't care."

"I think you're wrong," I said. "I've spent quite a bit of time with him and he's very upset."

"About me, maybe," she said. "But he doesn't care about Bruce. That hasn't changed."

I looked at Erica.

"Would you all leave me alone, please?" Mrs Wilson said. "Just for a few minutes. I don't want you all standing here scaring Bruce."

Mrs Lennox said to no one in particular, "I'll be inside," and headed back to the school. Bet she was glad to get away from the madness.

"Want to wait in the car?" I asked Erica.

28.

I told Erica about the talk I'd had with Dr Snow.

"You shouldn't have let Clare pay the ransom," Erica said.

I shook my head. "Not my choice to make."

"Next time, Bruce won't come back."

"You sure he'll come back this time?"

Erica tapped the side of her head with a couple of fingers. "There's no doubt in that poor woman's mind," she said. "So I'm sure Bruce will walk round that corner any minute."

She was right.

Bruce arrived about five minutes later.

I saw Mrs Wilson run down the nearly empty street.

All of a sudden I saw her stop, fling her arms around thin air and swing her invisible child off the ground.

"Something else, isn't it?" I said.

"That's love," Erica said. "Blind,

screwed-up, mad as a bag of squirrels. But it's love. Do you love your children like that?"

"I don't need to," I said. "My kids are alive."

"Ain't you the lucky one," Erica said. She picked up her radio. "What's Dr Snow's number?"

29.

"I got a message telling me there was a change of plan," Mrs Wilson said later.

What was left of the day's sun crept through the sitting room window, drew a line across the floorboards and came to a stop just short of her feet.

Before we'd driven her home, she'd shown us where she'd dropped off the money. It was a dead-end five minutes away from the school. The kidnapper had told her to stuff the bag behind a couple of red trade waste bins. That was about an hour before we got there, and by the time we arrived, the money was gone. We left some officers

84

checking the area in case anybody had seen it being picked up.

I'd spoken to my uncle about ten minutes back. I thought he would say it was time he spoke to Mrs Wilson himself. But he said he trusted me. He said that I knew the mother and she was happy to talk to me, so there was no point in having to get her to trust him when I'd done that already.

I was doing fine, he said. And Erica was there now to hold my hand.

He wasn't sure about the shrink, though.

Dr Snow had come right away. And my uncle was wrong. She'd already helped out by taking Bruce to his room to play. She had clump-clump-clumped up the stairs with her walking stick, Les a couple of steps behind her. At first Mrs Wilson was too scared to let Bruce out of her sight, but it was the only way we could talk properly. Bruce's kidnapper hadn't hurt him, she said, which was something.

"How did the kidnapper contact you?" I asked. "Was it another note? A phone call? Text message? Email?"

After a minute Mrs Wilson answered my question. "It was a phone call."

"On your landline?"

She nodded.

"Have there been any calls since?"

"I don't know."

I had rung Les, but on his mobile. It was a long shot, but worth a try.

"Erica, would you check?" I asked. "See when the last call came in and if there's a number?"

"The phone's by the window," Mrs Wilson said.

Erica went off to try it.

"Carry on," I said to Mrs Wilson.

"The man told me I had to sneak away," she said. "Deliver the money this afternoon. And if I told anybody, or anybody followed me ..." She cleared her throat. "He said there would be a real finger in the post."

"Was it your own idea to dump your car?"

"No, he told me to. He said you'd be looking for it."

"Tell me about his voice," I said.

"From around here," she said. "Middle-aged." She shook her head. "Nothing that stood out."

Erica came back.

"Any luck?" I asked.

"It was a public phone," she said. "We might find CCTV."

I wouldn't bet on it. This guy was too smart.

It seemed Mrs Wilson agreed.

"You're not going to catch him, are you?" she said.

30.

I couldn't believe I was doing this.

It was Mrs Wilson's idea. And of course it made sense to her.

She'd sent Erica upstairs to get Bruce. Erica came back with Dr Snow and Les.

The shrink came up to me, her walking stick hardly hitting the ground. She grabbed my arm and dragged me over to the corner of the room. Erica must have told her what Mrs Wilson was planning.

"This is a terrible idea," she said. "You have to stop her."

"How?" I waited a second or two but she didn't say anything. "You're the expert," I said. "Show me."

Dr Snow clumped over to Mrs Wilson. I followed, standing close by so I could hear what they were saying.

"Bruce has been through a lot," Dr Snow was saying. "I don't think he wants to talk about it."

"You don't think it might help him to tell us what happened?" Mrs Wilson asked.

"No, I think it'll make it harder for him."

"Bruce says he's fine." Mrs Wilson lifted her arm into the air and curled it round, just about the height of a child's shoulders. "Somebody needs a haircut, I think," she said. She was smiling as she looked up again. "He doesn't mind telling us."

"But I don't think – "

"Bruce is going to tell us, Dr Snow. It doesn't matter what you think."

Dr Snow nodded, shook her head, then moved off to take a seat on the corner of the sofa.

31.

"What do you want to ask Bruce?" Mrs Wilson asked me.

I wasn't sure where to look. After a second I became aware that I was scratching my eyebrow over and over. And it wasn't even itchy.

"Shouldn't you get your notebook out?" Mrs Wilson asked.

I did as Mrs Wilson said. At least it gave me something to do with my hands.

"Could you ask Bruce if he can describe the kidnapper?" I said.

Mrs Wilson turned her head and whispered something to the air. Then she said to us, "Bruce had a blindfold on. He didn't see the man."

We didn't speak for a while.

"What else?" Mrs Wilson asked.

"What about at the school? Didn't Bruce see him then?"

Mrs Wilson whispered again.

"He was tall," she said.

"What was he wearing?" Erica asked.

Mrs Wilson leaned down. "A suit," she said.

"What colour?" I asked.

"Grey."

"How old was he?"

"Bruce says he was older than Mummy."

The questions went on for about ten minutes. Ten very long minutes.

"That's great," Erica said at last. "But I think we need to get back to the station now."

32.

In the car, Erica said, "I don't know if I want to laugh or cry."

33.

When I sat down at my desk in the CID office, I saw the drawer was open.

"Some arsehole's been fiddling with my stuff," I said to Erica.

I spotted something in the drawer that I hadn't seen before. A piece of purple card. I pulled the drawer out.

There was a plastic pouch on one side of the cardboard. Inside was a plastic cut-off finger. Or there had been one, only now the plastic was torn away and the finger was gone.

Erica put her hand into the drawer and picked up a magazine. It was one I'd never seen before. A sailing magazine. She flicked through it and some pages fell out. There were words missing from the headlines. Some scraps landed on the desk – the missing words, with one or two letters cut out.

"Shit," Erica said. "What else have you got in there?" She stuck her hand back in the drawer.

"It's Dutton," I said. "Up to his usual tricks. Thinks it's funny."

Erica held up a brick of cash. "That's not usual." It was a tight little bundle of crisp new fifties. "How in the name of Christ did you get this, Collins?"

When I looked around the room, I saw that all my colleagues were watching me, looking for an answer.

I swallowed. My throat hurt.

34.

They put me in a holding cell downstairs. Not because of what was in my desk, but because I kicked the crap out of Sergeant Dutton.

I'd sprinted to his office, flung open the door and laid into him. He couldn't run away. There wasn't enough room. I pinned him to the wall and flung punch after punch at his fucking moustache.

They'd taken me down here to calm down.

I'd had some time to think. I don't know how long because they took my watch. Felt like a couple of hours since the door closed. I thought at least Erica would have come down to see me, but no, nobody came. It was just me and a dirty toilet and a bed.

I sat on the thin foam mattress in its blue, wipe-clean plastic cover and rubbed my sore hands. I tried to figure out why Dutton had framed me. Was it just because he blamed me for his wife leaving him?

I looked up when I heard a key in the lock. After a second or two, the door opened.

"Erica," I said. "Get me out of here."

"How could you do this?" she asked. She stepped right up to me. "Holly's gutted. And your kids, what do you think it's going to be like for them now?"

I couldn't believe I was hearing this. "Erica," I said, "what the hell are you talking about?" I put my hand on her arm.

She raised her fist. "Get the fuck off me!"

I put my hands in the air as if she was holding a gun. "What's wrong? It's Dutton. He set me up."

"I always thought you were a piece of shit, you know that?" Erica said.

"Listen to me," I said.

"Fuck you." She turned around, slammed the door shut behind her.

I walked over to the door and leaned my head against it. I stayed there for quite a while.

35.

I was back on the bed, perhaps half an hour later, when I heard footsteps outside. The key scraped in the lock again and my uncle stepped into the cell.

"Thank Christ," I said.

"You sure you don't want to see a Police Federation representative?" he asked.

"For beating up Dutton? Everybody

knows he was asking for it."

"Come with me," my uncle said.

I didn't need to be asked twice.

36.

Interview room 2. I knew it well. But I'd never sat on this side of the desk before. The room looked different when you were facing the door.

They'd left me there with a Uniform to keep an eye on me. He was under orders not to speak to me. That was fine. I didn't feel much like talking.

My uncle walked in carrying a briefcase. A grey briefcase.

"Seen this before?" he asked as he dumped it on the desk.

I checked to make sure and, yes, the name of Mrs Wilson's bank was there in gold letters on the front. "Where did you find it?" I asked. "Was the money – ?"

"I asked you if you've seen this before!" he shouted.

What the hell had got into him? "Yes," I said. "I have."

The door opened and Erica came in. She was carrying a large plastic bag filled with cash. Piles of it. As she got closer, I saw that the notes were 50s, and they were all held in bricks by rubber bands.

"Jesus," I said. "You did find it! Is it all there?"

"There's 120 grand," my uncle said. He took the bag from Erica and set it on top of the briefcase. "With the £5,000 we found in your desk, that's exactly half of Mrs Wilson's missing money. Where's the rest?"

"How would I know?" I asked.

"There's no point carrying on this game any more, Collins," Erica said, and folded her arms.

I folded my arms too. "Look, for the tenth time," I said, "Dutton's the man you want. He set me up."

"I'll grant you," my uncle said, "he might have been able to put that funny finger and those magazines in your desk. He might have put a stray five grand in your desk too. But do you think Dutton's the kind of guy who'd stick 120 grand in the boot of your wife's car?"

The words struck my kneecaps like hammers. I let down my head, put my hands flat on the desk.

"Holly found it and called me," Erica said. She leaned over and I felt her breath on my ear. "You make me puke," she said.

I stared at the bag of cash. "I have no idea how the money ended up in Holly's car." My mouth was dry. I licked my lips but it didn't help. "Dutton must have put it there."

"Here's the thing," my uncle said. "DS Dutton was in court yesterday, as a witness. He didn't leave until 3pm. The money was gone by then. He couldn't have lifted it. Would have been fucking impossible."

"It wasn't me." I wanted to stand up but I didn't think I'd be able to. "If I'd stolen the money, I'd have put it somewhere safe."

"Where?" my uncle asked. "We're still missing half of it. Tell us where it is. If we don't get all the money back, you're well fucked, sunshine."

I didn't say anything.

"Well?"

"Better get me that Police Federation representative," I said.

37.

Back in the holding cell, it was just me and the mustard-yellow walls.

I was a detective. I could work this out.

I'd been set up.

I just needed to prove that I was innocent.

The easiest way to do that was with an alibi.

The finger. Where was I when the finger was posted in Mrs Wilson's letterbox? Holly had gone to bed and the kids were out ...

I'd gone for a drive.

OK, that was no help.

The ransom money. I couldn't have picked up the money because ... shit. I was asleep in my car.

For God's sake. I couldn't prove a thing. I had to admit, if I was working this case, I'd think I was guilty.

I needed to find out who had set me up. Whoever it was had a pass for the CID office. Which meant that one of those bastards I worked with had framed me.

All I knew for sure was that it wasn't Dutton.

There wasn't much to go on, but I did have a few suspects.

I put a list together in my head. Everybody I could think of. And I started going through them, one by one.

After all, I had nothing else to do for a while.

Part Two
James

38.

Detective Inspector James Fleck didn't often take his wife out for dinner. It was the old bag's birthday but still she gave him a look of total shock when he told her she'd have to dress up tonight because they were going out somewhere posh.

He had to admit, he liked that look.

He picked up the his fourth or fifth pint and downed the dregs. Gave the waiter a nod and held up the empty glass. Good. Another one on the way.

Sarah looked at him, eyes narrowed. That was her 'you've-had-too-many' look.

"Last one," he said. "Then an early night?"

Once upon a time, he'd fancied the arse off her. Still did, after a few pints. And his back was fine today. The new treatment had made a difference in just a few days. You got what you paid for.

Before he'd left for work that morning,

he'd given Sarah a card and a clothes voucher for ten quid. For a laugh.

She'd opened it and tried to look happy. She had pecked Fleck on the check and said, "Wish you could do something for Frank. That'd be a great present."

And Fleck had said he was doing all he could, but it looked bad. Their poor nephew had been caught red-handed cheating a mad woman. He should just admit it.

What Fleck didn't tell her was that Frank seemed to be cracking up, which was a nice wee bonus. The jumped-up little toss-pot couldn't stop his own wife from shagging another bird, so he'd taken it out on Dutton. Made Dutton's wife leave him.

There was no call for that.

The lad had no moral core. Deserved what was coming to him. Every sweaty inch of it.

So later that morning, as Fleck's wife was closing the front door behind him, he'd turned back and said, "Oh, almost forgot." And then he told her they'd be eating out for dinner.

But that wasn't the end of the presents. He had one more to give her now. Maybe it would help him get his leg over later.

He tucked his hand inside his jacket pocket. Pulled out an envelope.

Sarah dabbed her mouth with her napkin as she watched him.

He handed the envelope to her. "Happy birthday."

"But you've already given – "

"Shut up and open it."

She didn't need to be told twice. She tore open the envelope and took out the tickets. "Oh, my good God, James!" She put her hand over her mouth. "Oh, good God."

She'd always wanted to go on a cruise. Fuck, it might even be fun. He'd always liked the sea. Missed his boat. Saddest day of his life having to sell her. Worse than having to sell one of your own kids.

"But can we afford this?" she asked. "Where did the money come from?"

He turned his empty pint glass around, then said, "You won't like it if I tell you."

"You've been gambling!"

"How many times ...?" He looked across at her. "I don't gamble." He paused. "But maybe I did have a wee bet."

"One of those value bets?"

"You've got it in one. I saw odds I liked. Took the risk." He smiled. "And it paid off."

"You always said it would. Over time."

"And you always said I was wrong," he reminded her.

"That's because you always lose."

"Well, not this time."

"You smug bastard, James." She smiled. "How much did you win?"

"Enough to pay for the cruise." And then some. The cruise cost six grand. Which left him with precisely 119 grand.

"How much?" she asked again.

"Just what you've got there," he lied. "Plus a couple of grand spending money."

"You've spent it all on me?"

"On us," he said.

Sarah leaned forward and kissed him. "Sometimes," she said, "you can be a very nice man."

Also by Allan Guthrie...

Kill Clock

The kill clock is ticking...

Pearce's ex-girlfriend is back. She needs twenty grand before midnight. Or she's dead.

She doesn't have the money. Nor does Pearce. And time's running out.

Fast...

www.barringtonstoke.co.uk